I0684358

Next Exit

David R. Beshears

Novella adapted directly from the
screenplay

Large Print Edition

Greybeard Publishing
Washington State

Greybeard Publishing
P.O. Box 480
McCleary, WA 98557-0480

ISBN 978-1-947231-17-7
(large print edition)

Next Exit

Chapter One

The motel and café sat alone on a lonely highway. The sign atop the tall pole high above the gravel parking lot read "Jan's Motel and Café". The building at one end of the motel was two-storey, with the lobby/office on the first floor, the owner apartment on the second. There were eight motel rooms along the single-storey row extending from the office. A wooden deck ran the length of the row of rooms, the walkway starting at the breezeway between the office and motel room number one.

The companion café was the square building on the other side of the motel office. A handful of large windows were set into the front of the building.

There was no traffic on the isolated highway. The landscape surrounding the motel and highway was empty, desolate. The world was quiet, was still but for a thin cloud of dust drifting slowly across the lot.

Mother sat at the large picture window of the owner apartment above the office, overlooking the motel parking lot below. She was in her seventies, but could have passed for anywhere from seventy to a hundred years old. She was Asian, dressed conservatively. Her dark hair was streaked with gray, was combed and neat.

She was sitting in a high-backed chair before the window, looking outward, unmoving, betraying no emotion. On the TV tray beside her was a water glass, a plate of cookies and several prescription bottles. The apartment behind her was open concept, with fuzzy light streaming in through the window and into the room. A couch and several chairs were in the middle of the room, encircling a large coffee table.

A door in the back wall opened to a small hall leading to the back rooms of the apartment. The kitchen was visible through an open arch beside the hall door.

The apartment, as the world of the motel, was quiet, still.

Reuben was steering his delivery truck down a two-lane highway, an unbending, pale asphalt ribbon running across a desolate landscape. He was in his thirties, dressed in Khaki pants and a long-sleeved shirt. His dark hair was combed neat. He had an obvious Hispanic background.

Reuben's vehicle was a cab-over with a twenty-four foot box. The cab interior was clean and uncluttered but for a clipboard of paperwork sitting on the dash. There were no other vehicles on the road. The only sound was the loud hum of the truck's engine set against the rumble of truck tires rolling across the asphalt.

He glanced at his mirrors, then briefly outward at the barren landscape on either side of the empty highway. A sign then up ahead on the right: "Food and Lodging Next Exit". Twenty seconds later, a sign with an arrow and the word "Exit".

Rueben slowed the truck and took the exit.

This highway was narrower than the last and there was an even greater sense of isolation. Traveling the road for a short distance, ahead on the right, Reuben saw the familiar old sign on a tall pole: "Jan's Motel and Café".

Approaching, the motel and café buildings were visible, set far back from the road, across a large gravel parking lot.

Rueben put on the right turn signal, slowed the truck, pulled into the parking lot.

§

Mother, sitting in her window, watched Reuben walking from his parked truck toward the café. Her expression remained unchanged.

Jan came into the main room from the back of the apartment. She was a middle-aged Asian woman, dressed in comfortable work pants and shirt, her hair pulled back out of the way. She was carrying a laundry bag.

She stopped midway to the front door and spoke to her mother-in-law.

"Mother," she said. "I'll be back in an hour."

Mother said nothing out loud, but Jan appeared to listen, responded.

"Of course. Lee is downstairs," she said, again waited. "Mother. Mother, do you need anything?"

Mother remained silent. Her expression didn't change.

"Very well," said Jan. "I'll be back soon, then."

She went to the door and left the apartment. The quiet returned.

Mother continued her silent watch.

Reuben entered the café. Large windows set into the wall beside the front door let in natural light. Hanging from the ceiling were several old light fixtures and a slow-spinning fan. There were half a dozen tables in the middle of the room. On a smaller table set against one wall were several school books, notebooks and other school articles.

The lunch counter was at the back of the room. A '*food-up*' window was set into the wall behind the counter; the clean, brightly lit kitchen was visible through the opening.

Sarah moved among the tables, setting out salt & pepper shaker sets and napkin holders. She was a Caucasian woman in her thirties, long hair pulled back from her face.

She smiled in Reuben's direction as she continued preparing for the day.

"Good morning, Reuben," she said. "How are things in the outside world?"

"You wouldn't recognize it, Sarah." He moved to one of the tables and took a seat.

Sarah called in the direction of the kitchen.

"Reuben regular, Samuel," she said.

"Reuben regular," said Samuel from the kitchen. "Already on it."

Samuel was a sixty year old black man, a retired Coast Guard cook. He was dressed neat, kept himself as clean as he kept his kitchen.

Sarah brought a carafe and a cup from the coffee station over to Reuben's table. Reuben watched her set the cup on the table in front of him.

"When did you last take a day off, Sarah?"

"Been a while, for sure," she said absently, filling his cup. "Yourself?"

"Oh, you know me."

"Oh, that I do." Sarah started back to the coffee station behind the counter.

"I can take you away from all this, Sarah," said Reuben to Sarah's receding figure.

"I like it here."

"I'll have you back day after tomorrow."

"Sorry," said Sarah, giving Reuben a wink. "Obligations prevent me from saying yes."

"Boy, howdy, do I get that."

Reuben took a swallow of his coffee, carefully set his cup down in from of him. He glanced in the direction of the small table against the wall with the school materials, then about the café.

"You work seven days a week, study during your breaks, you school online, and you live out of a motel room. Sarah, you really do need to see the outside world for yourself."

"I don't have a car," she stated matter-of-factly.

Reuben leaned back in his chair.

"And so my offer, dear lady."

"Uh-huh. Thanks just the same."

Samuel set a breakfast plate into the 'food-up' window.

"Reuben regular, up," he called out from the kitchen.

Sarah gave Reuben another wink as she turned about to get his plate.

Jan pushed the housekeeping cart along the walkway that ran the length of the eight rooms. She had already passed several of the rooms on her way to room 8 at the end of the row. She would start there and work her way back.

The only sound was that of the cart's wheels rolling across the wood deck of the walkway.

She passed the door with the number '3' on it.

She passed the door of Room 4. The curtain in the window beside the door shifted and began to part.

She spoke in the direction of the window as she continued past.

"Good morning, Mr. Bedford," she said.

In motel room number 4, Matthew Bedford was pushing aside the curtains, leaning over a small table that sat beneath the window. He could just see Jan's receding figure.

"Good morning, Jan," he said.

The room behind him was oversize, large enough for a double bed, dresser, desk and chair, a small couch and easy chair, as well as the table and chair at the window. The archway in the back wall opened to a small kitchenette with a two-burner stove, a refrigerator, sink and counter, and a chrome and Formica kitchen table with a single chair.

Matthew was forty years old, was dressed comfortably in slacks and a light shirt. He sat at the table, pushed his thick hair behind his ears. He looked down at his laptop as he prepared for his morning work session.

He briefly glanced outside. Reuben's delivery truck was visible across the lot. The café on the other side of the office wasn't visible from his window.

He noted then a mail truck just turning off the highway and coming into the parking lot.

Right on time...

He turned his attention back to his laptop.

Mike came into the café, looked about as he walked across the room, past Reuben eating his breakfast, and settled in at the lunch counter. He was wearing the gray-blue uniform of the postal service.

Sarah brought the carafe and a cup from the coffee station, stood behind the counter opposite Mike.

"How's your day startin' out, Mike?" She set the cup in front of Mike and filled it from the carafe.

"Just like every other, Miss Sarah." He picked up the cup, took a sip as he turned about, looked again about the room.

"How go the studies?" he asked.

"They go just fine, thanks," she said, then called back over her shoulder in the direction of the kitchen. "Mike regular, Samuel."

"On it," Samuel called back through the food-up window opening. "Mike regular."

Mike turned half-about on his stool, glanced again to Sarah's table with the school books.

"What ya' got, Sarah?" he asked. "One more year?"

"About that." Sarah had moved back to the coffee station.

Mike turned further into the room, looked to Reuben.

"Waddya think about that, Reuben?" he asked. "Won't be long, we'll have a PhD in our midst. Doctor Sarah."

"Sounds great," Reuben said wearily. He glanced briefly at Sarah. "They got an opening here for an Astrophysicist?"

"With a side of waitress," said Sarah.

"Reuben, what's the matter with you?" said Mike.

"Don't sweat it, Mike," said Sarah. "Just our friend's way of implying that I fear the outside world."

"Ah..." Mike took another sip of his coffee, turned back forward and set the cup on the counter. "And? Is that so?"

Sarah managed a sly smile. "I can telecommute."

"Ah," he said again. "Of course."

"She's serious," said Reuben.

"Of course," Mike said thoughtfully. He half-shrugged, lifted his cup and took

another sip, then a longer swallow. "Well...
this is a most pleasant environment, after
all. I might just move here myself."

Jan pushed the housekeeping cart back
along the walkway, past Room 1, before
stopping at the breezeway between the
row of rooms and the office. She lifted the
full laundry bag from the top of the cart
and walked through the breezeway, past
and behind the stairwell. She stepped
through an open door and walked into the
utility room.

Two large washing machines and two
large dryers sat in a row along the length of
the left wall. Shelves and cabinets were set
along the wall opposite the machines.

The janitor's room was through the door
at the other end of the room. Lee stepped
into the doorway wiping his hands with a
blue work towel, leaned against the door
jamb and looked over at his wife. Lee was

forty five, had strong Asian features, straight dark hair with streaks of silver. He was dressed in coveralls.

He tossed the towel behind him in the general direction of an unseen basket in the janitor's room.

"Jan," he said. "The shampooer is working."

"Thank you, Lee," she answered casually. "Mr. Howard's room this morning. Mr. Bedford's then, once he's finished his writing for the day."

"Yes, yes..." said Lee. "Samuel's room is done, is it not?"

"And Sarah's."

"Right." He watched as Jan pulled laundry from the bag and began filling one of the washing machines. He changed the subject, then. "Mother is anxious today."

Jan kept working, said nothing.

"Troubling," Lee continued. "Something..."

"Yes. Fretful," said Jan at last.

"You sensed it as well."

"She wasn't exactly hiding it, Lee." Jan measured detergent, poured it into the washing machine and closed the lid.

"No. Suppose not," he sighed. "Not her strong suit."

Jan turned on the washing machine.

"Supplies coming today," she said.

"I saw the schedule." Lee folded his arms across his chest, kept a shoulder against the jamb. "Mr. Howard is waiting for a package as well. He asked that we watch for it."

Jan started to leave the utility room, slowed at the door and spoke over her shoulder to her husband.

"Drop in on Mother now and then, will you?"

"Yes, ma'am," said Lee. "When I can."

Mother sat silent, unmoving, her focus on the world beyond the window in front of her. The water glass, plate of cookies and bottles of prescription pills sat untouched on the TV tray beside her.

She watched Reuben as he walked from the direction of the café toward his delivery truck. The road beyond the gravel parking lot was empty. The barren landscape on the other side of the road was empty.

The only movement was Reuben.

He reached the back of his truck, flipped open the latch and pushed up the door.

Mother watched...

Matthew sat at the window table in his room, worked at his laptop. He hesitated, stopped, leaned back in his chair. He lifted his focus from the laptop screen to look out the window.

Across the parking lot... a ramp was extended from the back of the Reuben's delivery truck. Reuben walked a hand truck down the ramp to the ground. The hand truck was stacked with boxes.

Matthew turned his focus again to his laptop, stared at the screen. He frowned, leaned forward and got back to work.

Mike slid off the lunch counter stool and took out his wallet. He pulled out two bills and set them on the counter.

"Well..." He took a final swallow from his coffee and set the empty cup on the money. "Swift completion of my appointed rounds and all that."

Sarah was sitting at her table with her school books. She looked briefly up from her studies.

"Thank you, Mike," she said. "See you tomorrow."

"I'll be here."

"Of course you will."

Mike called out in the direction of the kitchen.

"Later, Samuel," he said, and left the café.

Samuel came out of the kitchen, walked behind the counter. He brought a water pitcher and glass up from beneath the counter.

"So ends the morning rush," he said, speaking in Sarah's general direction. He came around the counter and sat on one of the stools. He faced the room, his back to the counter, and took a swallow of his water.

"You need anything?" he asked.

"I'm good. Thanks." Sarah kept writing in her notebook.

Samuel reached back behind him and set his glass on the counter.

"All right... back in thirty." He slid off the stool. "I'll be in my room."

Sarah glanced up at the clock, noted the time. She returned to her studies.

"Enjoy your show," she said absently. "Carol still winning?"

"Connie." Samuel was halfway across the room. "Seven days and counting. Three hundred and eight thousand and counting."

"Connie," Sarah mumbled. "Right."

"Names are important, Sarah. You're talking about the future Mrs. Smith."

"Perhaps introductions are in order," said Sarah, smiling as she focused on her schoolwork.

"I'm sure we'll get along just fine," Samuel replied on his way out.

Chapter Two

Mike entered the motel lobby, now carrying a canvas mailbag. The room was small, carpeted, with the check-in counter just three long steps from the door. An old cash register sat at one end of the counter, a small wire brochure rack at the other. There were only a handful of old brochures in the rack, and they appeared to have been there a long while.

A board with eight hooks was mounted on the wall behind the counter. Four of the hooks had room keys. An open door behind the counter led to the back office.

Lee came out of the office and stood behind the counter, still wearing his coveralls. He reached under the counter and brought out a cap with "US Postal Service" embroidered on it.

"Good morning, Mike." Lee put on the cap. "Whatcha got for us on this fine day?"

"Hey, Lee." Mike brought a stack of mail out of his bag, shuffled through it and read out names as he set envelopes and a small package on the counter. "Two letters for the distinguished Mr. Bedford, three for you and Jan… and a little something for Mr. Howard."

Lee picked up the letters and the package. He brought a wire basket up from under the counter and tossed the letters and the package into it.

"Thank you much, Mike." Lee returned the basket under the counter.

"Absolutely, sir." Mike adjusted his mailbag, then indicated Lee's coveralls. "So, whatcha workin' on?"

"Assorted small appliances."

"Sounds thrilling," said Mike.

"Such is the life of motel ownership."

Mike gave an appreciative glance around the lobby.

"I can't think of a better retirement, Lee," said Mike. "I envy you and Jan. I truly do."

"It's not so much retirement as a dramatic change in life direction."

Mike stepped from counter, started back to the door. He stopped midway and again looked appreciatively about.

"That change in direction... three years ago, wasn't it?" he asked.

"Three and a half," said Lee. He leaned on the counter.

"Right. Right," he said thoughtfully. "I remember that first day. Met you and Jan, thought the two of you were out of your minds; takin on a rundown motel and café, so far off the beaten path."

"Exactly what we were looking for."

"I see it now. I do." Mike reached for the door handle. "I'll see ya' tomorrow, Lee."

"We'll be here."

"Yes. I know that."

Lee watched Mike leave the lobby. He straightened, pushing off the counter. He looked about the lobby; his lobby.

His and Jan's...

Matthew stepped out of his room, closed the door behind him. He took a moment then to look casually about. He watched a vehicle traveling the road, some distance out.

Jan came out of the room next to his. She set a laundry bag atop the housekeeping cart, slipped a spray bottle into a side pocket.

"Are you finished for the day, Mr. Bedford?"

"Another day done, Jan," said Mathew. "And how goes your day?"

Jan placed her forearms atop the cart, clasped her hands.

"The morning chores are just about done," she said.

"I'll say it again," said Matthew, taking a stepped nearer. "You are too good to us, Jan."

"You all make my world a better place, Mr. Bedford. I appreciate you very much."

"And we, you. I hope you know that."

Jan smiled modestly. "Thank you."

They watched the vehicle out on the road turn into the parking lot. It moved slowly in the direction of the café. It was a sheriff's deputy vehicle, an older model sedan. The word "Sheriff" was written on the side.

"She's right on time," said Matthew.

"That she is."

Matthew made to start away. "I'm off, then."

Jan straightened as she too prepared to start away.

"I suppose I should get back at it, as well," she said. "Enjoy your lunch, Mr. Bedford."

"I thank you, Ma'am." Matthew stepped off the walk.

Jan watched Matthew walk toward the café for a moment, then she moved around behind the housekeeping cart and pushed it along the walkway.

Sarah carried a small tray of clean coffee cups from the kitchen. She talked with Samuel, unseen in the kitchen, as she began putting the cups away under the counter.

"Is the future Mrs. Smith still winning?" she asked.

Samuel appeared briefly in the food-up window as he went about cleaning.

"I'm afraid the wedding's off," he said.

"She lost, huh? Sorry to hear that."

A young black woman dressed in sheriff's deputy uniform came into the café.

Sarah spoke in the direction of the food-up window.

"Early lunch crowd, coming in." She walked from behind the counter with a glass and a water pitcher. "Hey, Charlene. Grab a table. How ya' doing? Ya' hungry?"

"Gotta tell ya', Sarah," said Charlene, "I find myself hungry every day about this time."

Sarah filled the water glass and set it on the table in front of Charlene.

"That would explain your arrival here on a daily basis at just about this time."

"Possibly..." Charlene spoke to the Sarah's receding figure. "But don't minimize the power of your magnetic personality, Sarah."

"*Aw, shucks, Deputy...*" Sarah stepped around behind counter, placed the water pitcher under the counter and called to the kitchen. "Feed your daughter, Samuel."

"Coming up," Samuel called, unseen. To Charlene, then: "Hey, baby."

"Hey, Dad," said Charlene. To Sarah then, in a faux whisper, "Don't tell Dad, but it's the cooking that brings me back day after day."

"Your secret is safe with me," said Sarah.

Matthew came into the café, started across the room to his favorite table. Seeing him settle in, Sarah began scooping ice cubes into a tall glass.

"Mr. Bedford. Did your morning go well?" Sarah filled the glass with iced tea and started around the counter.

"Very well, Sarah. And your studies?"

"Good. Mostly research these days. Interesting stuff." She set the iced tea on the table. "What'll you have today?"

"How's the clam chowder?"

"It would be a most excellent choice."

"Cup of chowder it is," said Matthew. "And a tuna sandwich on white."

"You got it, Matthew." Sarah started back to the counter, calling toward the kitchen. "Samuel... Matthew number three."

Samuel appeared briefly in the food-up window as he moved about the kitchen.

"Chowder and tuna sand, on the way," he said. He put a plate in the food-up window. "Charlene regular, up."

Matthew picked up his glass of iced tea, took a long swallow as he looked over at Charlene.

"How are you, Deputy Smith?" he asked her.

"I'm just fine, Mr. Bedford. You?"

"I'm doing just great."

"I finished your book last night," she said, a broad smile. "Loved the ending."

"Why, thank you, Charlene. That warms my heart."

"I downloaded the sequel," she said then. "Starting it tonight."

"Wonderful. I hope you enjoy it."

Sarah brought Charlene's lunch over, set the plate on the table in front of her.

"I liked it," she said. She gave a wink to Matthew. "My favorite author."

"That's very kind of you, Sarah." Matthew knew that Sarah had read most of his books.

"So, why is my favorite author keeping me waiting?" Sarah looked aside to Charlene. "Consider yourself fortunate, Charlene. How many books to go?"

Back to Matthew before Charlene had a chance to respond.

"Please, Matthew. Finish the book."

"Yes, Ma'am," said Matthew. "I'm on it."

Sarah turned again to Charlene. "He writes three and a half hours a day."

"I know that, Sarah."

"I mean, <u>exactly</u> three and a half hours. How does he expect to finish at three and a half hours a day?"

Charlene had no response.

Matthew took another drink from his iced tea.

"I sit in front of my laptop three and a half hours a day." He tapped at his temple, then. "But I'm writing all the time."

Sarah smiled, briefly placed a hand on Matthew's shoulder as she started back to the lunch counter.

"And I love you for it, sweetie," she said.

"Thank you, dear reader."

Charlene had started into her lunch, looked to Matthew.

"Working on book twenty two?" she asked.

"Something like that."

"I do have a lot of reading to do."

"And I much appreciate the effort, Deputy."

Mother was sitting at her window. Her casual attention was on the sheriff's deputy vehicle, parked near the café. The world outside was otherwise still.

Lee came into the apartment, carrying a cardboard box. He looked briefly over at Mother before taking the box into the kitchen. Coming back into the main room, he spoke in the direction of his mother, who kept her focus on the world beyond the window.

"Mother... is everything all right?" he asked.

He stood in the middle of the room. He waited.

Mother said nothing, did not speak aloud. She continued to look out the window.

"You seem a bit on edge is all," said Lee. "You will let us know? Mother?"

Mother watched as an old passenger bus pulled off the highway. It came to a stop in the middle of the parking lot. A few moments later, a woman stepped off, a small travel bag in hand. She was young, in her twenties, white.

Mother's head twitched slightly, as if in recognition.

Behind Mother, Lee turned about and started to the back of the apartment.

"Very well, Mother. I have to change," he said. Reaching the hallway, as if in response to something not spoken aloud, "Yes, yes..." he said. He was gone then into the bedroom.

Mother continued her focus beyond the window. Her attention closely followed the young woman as she walked in the direction of the motel lobby below. The bus behind her started away, leaving the parking lot.

Emily was young, slim, Caucasian, dressed in jeans and a long-sleeved button shirt. She came into the lobby, crossed the room in three steps and stood at the check-in counter. She set her travel bag on the floor beside her and waited.

Jan came out of the back office and approached counter. She was clearly taken aback.

"Emily," she stated stiltedly.

"Hello, Mom," she said, casual, calm. "Surprise..."

"Emily," Jan said again. "Is everything all right?"

"Sure. Why do you ask?" Emily seemed to enjoy her mother's discomfort.

"Well... because... what are you doing here?"

"Aren't you glad to see me?"

"Of course I am," Jan said, hesitantly. "But..."

The two fell silent then for several moments. Jan reached across and placed a hand on Emily's hand.

"I'm very glad you are here," she said.

"Thanks, Mom." Emily sounded genuine. "I hope there's a room available."

"Of course." Jan reached back and took the key for Room #7 from its hook. She placed it on the counter. "It's yours for as long as you like."

"Next door to Mr. Howard," said Emily, taking the key. She smiled. "Nice and quiet."

"They're all quiet, Emily," said Jan.

"True enough." Emily picked up her travel bag. "I think I'd like to settle in. A long trip, ya' know."

"Yes, yes," said Jan. "I'll let your father know you're here."

"We can get together later?"

"Yes, yes."

"Good." Emily took a step back, half-turned and prepared to leave the lobby. "Grandmother is well?"

"I believe she is expecting you," she said.

"Right." Emily glanced up, for just a moment, to the apartment above. "I expect so."

Jan watched Emily leave the office, the door slowly closing behind her. Jan took a step back, keeping a hand on the counter. She hesitated, turned about finally and went back into the office.

Matthew stood outside his room, quietly taking in the evening. The world was silent, unmoving; as always. The horizon was just showing sunset colors.

He heard a door opening, looked to his left. Emily had just come out of her room, was closing her door. She walked toward him, smiled and stood beside him.

She looked from Matthew to the view.

"Hello, Mr. Bedford," she said. "So good to see you."

"Hello, Emily. Matthew, please."

"Hello, Matthew. So good to see you."

"Right... you as well," Matthew sighed. "It's been a while. Visiting?"

"I haven't decided yet."

Matthew looked side-glance at Emily, but didn't want to miss the sunset.

"Sounds mysterious," he said.

"Yeah, well, that's me." Emily stepped off the walkway, looked back to Matthew. "Dinner?"

Matthew took a final look at the horizon, sighed again and stepped down to stand beside Emily.

"That's the plan," he said.

They started across the parking lot toward the café.

"I read your last book," said Emily.

"Yes? What'd you think of it?"

"It was okay," she said, hesitating. "You've done better."

They took another half dozen steps in silence.

"I always appreciated your honesty, Emily," he said. "So. It's been what? A year?"

"Fifteen months and a scattering of days."

"Ah..." Matthew managed a slight grin then. "It has been awfully quiet."

"No doubt," she said. "Kinda why I left."

Matthew looked over at Emily now and gave a knowing smile. He looked to the horizon as they continued walking. The sunset was in full bloom.

"Not quite the way I remember it," he said.

Now Emily put on the knowing smile and gave Matthew's earlier comment back to him.

"I always appreciated your honesty, Mr. Bedford."

"Matthew. Please."

Emily nodded in response.

Another few steps...

"I imagine your folks were glad to see you," said Matthew.

Emily's grin was genuine.

"Sure," she said.

§

Mother watched Emily and Matthew from her window as they walked across the parking lot toward the café. Jan was standing beside Mother, hands clasped, watching the same scene.

Beyond the glass, the sunset was in full bloom.

"She was exhausted after her trip, Mother," said Jan. "She went straight to her room."

Jan and Mother kept their focus on Emily as they watched her walk toward the café.

"Yes," said Jan. "I'm sure she will."

Lee came into the room from the back of the apartment. He stopped near the couch as he finished buttoning his shirt.

"Will Mother be joining us?" he asked.

"I'm afraid not," said Jan. "I'll bring a plate back for her."

"Mother? Are you sure?" asked Lee. "It has been such a long time. Everyone would love to see you."

Lee waited for her answer, nodded then. "All right, then." He turned to Jan. "Jan?"

Jan rested a hand on Mother's shoulder.

"I'll bring a plate back for you." She joined Lee and they left the apartment.

Mother continued to watch the evening beyond the window.

Sarah was setting a plate of food at Matthew's table when Matthew and Emily came into the café.

"Hello, folks," she said. "Dinner's about ready."

"Smells delicious," said Matthew as they approached the table. "What are we having? I smell fresh baked bread."

"Lasagna." Sarah started back to the counter, spoke to the food-up window.

"Another plate for Emily, Samuel," she said.

"Plate for Emily," said Samuel from the kitchen. "On it."

Sarah returned to the table with another place setting of napkin and silverware, glass of water. She set the items on the table in front of Emily.

"Emily, welcome," she said matter-of-factly. Her tone wasn't warm, neither was it cold."

"Hello, Sarah," said Emily. "How have you been?"

"Quite well. Thank you."

"School?"

"Going well," said Sarah. "Thank you."

Back at the food-up window, Samuel set two plates up. One was covered.

"Two up," he called out. "Mother to go. Plate for Emily."

Sarah started back to the counter and the food-up window.

Emily slid her chair back. "I'll take my grandmother's dinner to her," she said.

"Are you sure?" asked Sarah. "I can take it to her."

"I'm glad to do it, Sarah." Emily approached the counter. "Make my plate to go."

Jan and Lee entered the café. Jan called out to the kitchen.

"Mother's dinner to go please, Samuel," she said.

"Taken care of, Jan." Sarah finished wrapping Emily's plate, slid both plates across the counter. "Thank you, Emily."

Emily took the plates in hand and started back across the café. She passed Jan and Lee, who were working their way to the table directly beside Matthew's.

"I can take that, Emily," said Jan.

"No problem, Mom; my chance to sit with Grandmother."

"I'm sure she'll enjoy that." Jan continued then to the table.

Lee stopped and placed a hand on Sarah's arm.

"So good to see you, Emily," he said. "Talk with you later?"

"Sure, Dad. See you then."

Emily continued to the door and Lee joined Jan at their table. He looked across to Matthew at the other table as he sat down.

"Good evening, Mr. Bedford," he said.

"Good evening, sir," said Matthew.

Samuel put two more plates up in the food-up window.

"Lee and Jan up," he called out.

Mother was sitting at her window. Outside, the gray blanket of dusk lay across the parking lot and the desert-like landscape beyond the empty ribbon of highway. There was an iridescent glow to it all, and it shone on Mother's face.

The sound of the door opening broke the silence. Emily entered the apartment juggling two plates of food. She closed the door behind her with her foot.

"Hello, Grandmother." Emily set the plates on the coffee table. "Yes, Grandmother."

She took a chair from the living area, set it beside Mother's TV tray.

"I am sorry. It was a difficult trip," she said then, reaching for a second TV tray that was leaning against a wall. She opened the tray and put it in front of her chair. "I'm here now, Grandmother."

She retrieved one plate of food and set it on Mother's TV tray, moving the other articles aside.

"Do you mind if I join you for dinner?" she asked, uncovering the plate. She set the silverware beside the plate. "Wonderful. We can talk."

She retrieved the second plate.

"Of course I did. You know I did." She set her plate and silverware on the tray. "I wasn't able to visit before now."

She sat and uncovered her plate.

"No, I couldn't," she said. She picked up her fork, glanced over at Mother. "All set then, Grandmother. How about you?"

There was a long pause. Emily smiled warmly.

"I love you too, Grandmother," she said.

Mother slowly reached across, rested her hand on Emily's forearm. Her focus remained outward.

Emily placed a hand on her grandmother's.

She looked down then to the dinner plates.

"Lasagna," she said. "It smells wonderful."

Matthew took another bite of potato.

"Yellow Finn's, aren't they?" he asked Samuel. Matthew and Samuel were sitting at one table, Lee and Jan at the next. The tables had been moved nearer each other for their group dinner.

"Yes," said Samuel. He indicated Matthew's plate. "Do you like it?"

"Yellow, a great choice for gratin."

"I prefer them for gratin, for scallops, like that," said Samuel. "I can't always get them."

"You have such talent, Samuel." Matthew turned to Jan, then. "Don't ever let this one go, Jan."

"Of course not, Matthew. You are all bound to our community for all time."

Sarah came into the café, having delivered a plate to Mr. Howard. She walked to the dinner party and sat before a covered plate at the table with Matthew and Samuel.

"And how is Mr. Howard?" asked Matthew.

"Hungry, apparently." She lifted the cover from her plate, set the cover aside as she looked over to Samuel. "He sends his complements, Samuel."

"How very nice."

"A pleasant man, Mr. Howard," said Jan. "We are less that he is unable to join us."

"He could certainly add to our milieu, dear lady," said Matthew. "But despite his absence, our world is most wonderful."

"And he is always with us in spirit," said Samuel.

"That he is," said Matthew. He lifted his glass of milk to Jan. "All part of that fabric of our community."

"I like that," said Sarah.

"As do I," agreed Jan.

The café grew silent then for several moments as everyone focused on their dinner.

Sarah put down her fork, took a drink from her milk and then looked over to Jan and Lee at the other table.

"I was surprised to see Emily," she said. "Were you expecting her?"

"We were not," said Lee.

"A pleasant surprise," said Jan. "So nice to have her with us."

"It certainly is," Matthew agreed. He looked questioning then, "So, she's not sure if this is a visit or to stay. Or so she said."

"We haven't really had a chance to talk on that."

"Of course." Matthew hesitated. "She is here now. Right?"

There was an uncomfortable silence.

"I suppose that is so," Lee said at last.

Jan looked briefly to Lee, to those at the other table, to her dinner then.

"I'm sure she will let us know her plans soon enough."

Sarah stood outside the café. The night sky was clear, the world still. Samuel stepped out, closed and locked the front door. He stood then beside Sarah; together they took in the scene.

"A warm evening," said Sarah.

"Likely to be an uncomfortable night," said Samuel.

"A bit of a breeze," said Sarah, feeling just a hint of the breeze on her face. "Might help."

Samuel let out a low sigh as he stepped away from the café. "I expect not."

Sarah followed Samuel, moved up beside him as they started together toward the motel.

Across the parking lot... Matthew was a shadow walking along the row of rooms; an easy, casual pace.

"Matthew... right on schedule," said Sarah.

"A very organized man, is Matthew."

"Set your clock by him."

"S'pose that's so."

They watched Matthew reach his door, open it and enter into his room.

Samuel continued.

"Of course, the fact that we are here every evening to witness the end of his evening walk might say something about us as well."

Sarah took in the entire motel.

"It might say something about us all," she said.

Midway across the parking lot, Sarah glanced up at the large window of the apartment above the motel office. Mother's silhouette was set against the fuzzy glow of a dim light somewhere in the apartment.

"Interesting days ahead," Sarah said quietly.

Samuel gave a questioning side-glance to Sarah as they approached the row of rooms.

"Emily," Sarah said, answering his silent question.

"Yes," said Samuel. "Interesting."

Two more steps in silence.

"So, what do you think?" asked Sarah.

"About what?"

"Samuel..." Sarah droned. "What brought her back?"

"I have no way of knowing."

"Yeah..." Sarah sighed. "I just hope... wherever she was... that she hasn't..."

Sarah hesitated, let the comment drift.

"We can but hope," said Samuel.

They stepped up onto the walk. Samuel went to the Room #1 door, Sarah to Room #2. Both brought out their keys.

"Good night, Sarah," said Samuel.

"See you in the morning, Samuel."

They entered their rooms, the doors closed behind them...

The world again fell quiet and still. The parking lot, the ribbon of highway, the barren landscape across the highway, all shimmered silver in the moonlight beneath the black sky.

In the picture window of the owner's apartment above the office... Mother's unmoving silhouette.

Chapter Three

Jan came out of the bedroom just before dawn, tying her robe. She saw Mother sitting at the window. Outside, the day was just turning a bright gray.

"Mother... what are you doing up so early?" she asked, waited. "You weren't up all night, were you?"

She moved into the center of the room, brushed her hair back with her hand.

"I certainly hope not. You know it isn't good for you." She started toward the kitchen. "Let me fix you something."

Mother continued to stare outside. She tilted her head just slightly...

Outside...

Emily walked along the highway, beneath the early dawn sky, alone in the world. She turned off the road and started across the parking lot.

The motel / café before her sat alone in the otherwise desolate landscape. The sky turned steadily brighter, the eastern horizon slowly awash in orange and red.

Emily looked up to the large window of the upstairs apartment. She smiled, raised a hand and gave a slight wave.

Matthew came out of his kitchenette carrying his cup of coffee, dressed in lounge pants and an undershirt. He walked across his room to the door.

Stepping outside, he stood at the edge of the walkway. He took a sip from his coffee, looked over the rim of his cup, saw Emily walking across the parking lot toward the café.

§

Emily entered the café, started across the room toward the lunch counter. Samuel came out of the kitchen as she climbed onto a stool.

"Good morning, Emily," he said. "You're up mighty early."

"This, an observation from someone who is up and about, here to offer me greeting."

"You got me there." Samuel moved to the coffee station. "The coffee will be a few minutes yet."

Emily talked as she watched Samuel set about making coffee.

"How have things been with you, Samuel," she said. "Life here good for you?"

"Absolutely. I wouldn't be anywhere else."

Emily grew contemplative. "I suppose it would be tough to find a better place to put down roots."

"Is that what brought you back?" Samuel looked back to Emily. "You ready to put down roots?"

"I don't really know, Samuel."

"Is that so?" Samuel finished preparing the pot, turned and leaned on the counter. He looked carefully at the young woman. "Emily... what brings you home?"

Emily frowned a dark frown, held her hands out in front of her, clasped her fingers. She didn't answer.

"Should we be concerned? Should we expect..." Samuel lifted a hand, gave a slight indication to the world... *out there*.

Emily slowly put on a thin smile.

"Whatever may be coming, Samuel, 'tis not I bringing it down on our little piece of the universe."

"So there is something coming... we should be concerned..."

Emily's thin smile faded. She looked back Samuel to the coffee station.

"Is that coffee ready yet?"

Samuel gave her a dark, furrowed brow, looked briefly back to the brewing coffee, back to Emily.

"Another minute."

The morning sun spread a warm glow across the motel parking lot. Reuben pulled his truck to a stop in front of the café and turned off the engine. He climbed down from the cab.

Emily came out of the café. She gave Reuben only a brief nod as she started across the lot toward the motel. He watched her for a few moments before heading for the café.

Sarah finished cleaning a table, walked toward the counter. Behind her, Mike and Reuben were sitting at separate tables, eating their breakfasts as they talked back and forth.

Mike took a swallow from his coffee, set the cup down beside his breakfast plate.

"I tell you, Reuben," he said. "One of these days I'm going to show up here with a suitcase rather than a mailbag... and never leave."

"It's pleasant enough. That's for sure," said Reuben, placating. He brought up a forkful of food. "Though it may be too quiet for me."

"Oh, I am so ready for the quiet, my friend. Morning here is tonic for my soul."

Sarah walked behind the counter, placed her cleaning supplies under the counter. She spoke to Mike and Reuben without actually looking in their direction.

"Mornings here are quiet by design, friends," she said.

Reuben took another forkful of food, chewed as he pointed his empty fork to Sarah.

"Plenty of time for your studies," he said, then took another forkful of his breakfast.

Sarah placed her forearms on the counter, clasped her hands and looked across the room.

"Yes, a happy secondary benefit," she said.

Lee stood at the window of the lobby, holding a coffee cup, quietly taking in the view, the morning, the quiet.

He took a sip of the coffee. He took a long sigh.

Jan came into the lobby from the back office, wiping her hands with the hand towel she was carrying. She moved behind the counter.

"Ah. Lee. There you are." She absently folded the towel, placed it on a shelf beneath the counter. "Is everything all right?"

Lee hesitated, frowned as he continued looking out at the midmorning.

"Sure," he said flatly. "I guess."

Jan came around and leaned back against the counter, always with an eye on Lee.

"I'm sure it'll work out," she said, folding her arms. "I really believe that."

"Oh, it'll work out. What form that takes, what it will mean for us..." He frowned again, shook his head. "No. No doubt we'll be fine."

"All right," said Jan. "So?"

Lee took another long swallow of his coffee.

Jan waited.

Lee furrowed his brow as he continued facing the window.

He looked down at his cup.

"I trust that Emily isn't bringing them down on us."

"As do I," said Jan.

The world beyond the window was still. The morning gray was gradually turning bright.

"Whatever her reason for coming home, she is home," he said. "For now, for however long. To stay or no…"

"She will tell us her reasons soon enough," said Jan. "What she intends."

"I'm sure." Lee thought long before continuing. "Mother is… concerned."

"Is she? She was up very early this morning. I think she may have been up most of the night." Jan pushed away from the counter. "Did she say anything to you? She was all mum to me."

"No. But I can feel it," said Lee. "All around me. All around us."

"Well, she's your mother."

Lee took another long breath, turned half about then and looked back at Jan.

"Is she?" There was a visible withdrawal in Jan.

"You know what I mean."

Lee finished his coffee, looked down at his empty cup. He turned back to the window.

"I sense... change." He shook his head, slowly. "Shifting shadows..."

Jan looked to Lee's silhouetted figure with some concern, held her silence.

Lee then, his focus beyond the window, "Where is Emily this morning?" he asked.

Midmorning light streamed in through the windows of the café; the ceiling fans slowly turned. Sarah was sitting at her table along the wall, studying. She glanced up at the sound of the door opening and closing. Charlene stepped into the middle of the room.

"Morning, Charlene," said Sarah, returning to her studies. "How goes the day?"

"Fine, Sarah." Charlene looked in the direction of the food-up window. "My dad?"

"He's out back, taking a break," said Sarah. "You're a bit early."

"I'm not really sure that five minutes qualifies as early." Charlene started in the direction of the kitchen. "Except here, I suppose."

She continued through the kitchen to the back door. She opened the door to the sound of the muffled squeal of hinges and stepped outside.

The day was clear and warm. Samuel was sitting in one of two chairs along the wall beside the back door in a cool shadow. He had a glass of water in hand.

Charlene let the door close behind her to the same squealing hinges. She looked out across the barren landscape, moved then to sit in the empty chair beside her father.

"Morning, Dad," she said.

"Good morning. Did the outside change their clocks?"

"Wow," she groaned. "What is it with you people?"

"Something in the air, I expect." He took a drink from his glass of water. "Good to see you. How's things?"

"Quiet. As always." She looked absently about. "Though out there isn't nearly as quiet as in here."

"Just the way we like it."

"I know," said Charlene. "Don't I know it."

"You never seemed bothered by the quiet. You never complained, anyway."

"I liked having my dad back full time," she said. "No more watching you heading off to sea for weeks at a time."

"Coast Guard was good to us," said Samuel. "I do like this better."

"Way lonely at first. I was glad when the others started moving in."

"So you were." Samuel takes a drink from his glass. "Speaking of neighbors, how's your new apartment?"

Charlene put on a half-grin.

"Quiet."

Samuel nodded. "Right."

He leaned forward then, slowly stood up. He took a final look outward, drank the last of his water.

"Well... break's over." He gave a wink to Charlene, walked to the door. "We got customers coming."

Charlene stood to follow him. "Don't want to be late for the rush."

Mike came into the lobby, his mailbag strap slung over his shoulder. He stood at the counter for several long moments before Lee finally came into the room from the back office.

"Hey, Mike." Lee reached under the counter and brought out his US Postal Service cap. "What ya' got for us today?"

Mike pulled two envelopes out of his mailbag.

"This morning we have two items for you and Jan, and..." double-checking his bag, "... and that's it."

Lee took the letters from Mike, brought out his basket and tossed the letters in. He returned the basket under the counter.

"I thank you, Mike."

"I'm here to serve, Lee."

"As are we all."

"That is a fact," Mike sighed. He leaned against the counter. "So... I understand Emily is back."

"You understand correctly," Lee said guardedly.

Mike hesitated, then spoke tentatively, "So... how's that going?"

"It goes well enough."

"Good, good." Mike pushed slowly from the counter. "And... so, do we know what brings her back, you know, home?"

"I expect she's just visiting."

"You really think so?"

"She hasn't said different."

"Right." Mike stepped away from the counter, took another step toward the door. "You'll let us know if that changes."

"Sure. Not a problem." Lee leaned against the counter, watched Mike give a good-bye nod and open the door.

He stared after the closing door.

The motel lobby fell quiet; a hollow, enclosing silence.

The day was warm. Emily was sitting in a folding chair beneath the window outside her motel room. She took in the world of the motel, studied the landscape that was spread out before her.

Matthew came out of his room, looked over at Emily as he closed his door. He stepped over to stand beside her, leaned against the wall and folded his arms. Together they took in the silence.

"Are you enjoying your visit?" asked Matthew.

Emily's expression showed that she understood where the question was coming from.

"I am," she stated. "Thank you for asking."

They again fell silent. This lasted for a few long seconds.

"I expect your grandmother is glad to see you."

"That she is."

More silence then.

"Your parents have made quite a nice place here," said Matthew. "You have to be of a certain character, but for those of us who have chosen to live here, we have a home."

"I would never argue that."

"No." Matthew grinned. "I suppose not."

Emily leaned back in her chair, felt the warmth of the day seep into her bones. The slight breeze brushed across her face and kept the afternoon from getting too hot.

"You know," Emily started then. "When we left the facility, snuck out in the dark of the night, I never in a million years expected to end up in a place like this."

"They gave up a lot for you, Emily," said Matthew.

Emily sa d nothing. There really was no response to that.

Matthew continued.

"I understand they were unhappy with the direction the research had taken, what little I know of it, but in the end, it was their concern for you. And for your grandmother."

"I know that, Matthew," said Emily. "I never meant to hurt them."

"I suppose not." Matthew frowned. "Not my place, I guess."

"No it isn't." Emily looked side-glance at Matthew, again looked forward. "I know you care for them."

"Yes, well… they've made a nice place here."

"So I've heard."

They fell silent once more, taking in the scene before them; Emily sitting in her chair, Matthew standing beside her, his back against the wall, arms folded.

Samuel was working in the kitchen, near the back of the room. Reuben had made a delivery earlier in the day and Samuel was unpacking the stack of boxes and transferring the large cans to the stock shelves along the back wall. A folding chair was propping the back door open, revealing daylight outside.

A shadow appeared in the open doorway. Samuel glanced briefly at the shadow before lifting another can from the box.

"Charlene. What brings you back?" He took the can over to the shelf. "Is everything all right?"

Charlene stepped fully into the room, stood beside the stack of cardboard of boxes. Seeing the top box was empty, she lifted it from the stack and set it aside.

"Everything's fine." She watched her dad take a box knife to the next box in the stack. "Found myself in the neighborhood." She shrugged, then. "Not like there's a lot happening out there."

Samuel opened the box, lifted out a can. He looked at it as he turned back to the shelf.

"There's never a lot happening out there," he said.

"Suppose so." Charlene rested her arms on the box. "I can take my break anywhere."

"Uh, huh…"

Samuel continued restocking the shelves from the delivered boxes. Charlene absently watched her dad work, her mind on something else.

"Dad…" she said at last.

"Daughter..." Samuel continued working.

"Dad..." she said again, hesitated again. Finally then, "Dad, have I changed?"

"Waddya mean, changed? I certainly hope so. You grow, you learn, you experience life. Change."

"But have my experiences made me *different*? Since, you know, moving out; moving away from the motel."

Samuel stopped working, stood opposite the stack of boxes from Charlene.

"Different?" he asked. "Not so I've noticed. Why do you ask?"

"I sometimes feel different," she said. "I feel... outside."

Samuel rested his arms across the top of the boxes.

"Ah. No longer '*one of us*'..."

"The more time I spend out there, the less I feel a part of in here."

Samuel furrowed his brow, took a few moments to think on his daughter's situation.

"I respected your decision to work and live outside, Charlene," he said. "It was a good decision, the right decision for you. Don't second guess it now."

"It's not that, Dad. But..." She struggled with where to take her thoughts.

"I see." Samuel slowly followed those thoughts. "Charlene, relationships change. They evolve. But never doubt, while you may be Deputy Smith out there, in here you will always be Charlene."

"Always *one of us*?"

"Always." Samuel straightened, lifted two cans from the box. "Now get out of here. Get back out there and do deputy sheriff stuff. I have work to do."

Charlene smiled awkwardly, backed away from the stack of boxes.

"Of course." She moved into the doorway. "I'll see you tomorrow."

"I'll be here."

Samuel was again alone. He returned to his work restocking his shelves. He glanced once to the open doorway, his smile fading, his expression considered.

He took another two cans from the box and carried them to the supply shelf.

Late afternoon was sliding into early evening. The deputy sheriff vehicle was parked along the side of the deserted highway. Charlene was sitting on the hood of the car, her feet resting on the bumper. She was looking up the road, empty of traffic. The 'Food and Lodging Next Exit' sign was a few hundred yards ahead.

She took a drink from a water bottle, continued to absently look up the road. Far behind her, near the highway vanishing point, a dark silhouette began to form... a vehicle.

Slowly pushing in on the silence then... the faint, distant sound of the approaching vehicle.

The silhouette took shape. The car continued to approach.

The sound of the vehicle grew steadily louder.

Charlene took another swallow from her water bottle.

The scene ahead of her flickered then. The image shuddered in and out; back.

The Next Exit sign shimmered out of existence.

The vehicle passed Charlene. She watched it continue up the road.

The sound of the vehicle faded into the encroaching silence.

Charlene was again alone.

The scene ahead flickered again, the image shuddered in and out again.

The 'Food and Lodging Next Exit' returned, several hundred yards ahead.

Charlene casually took another swallow from her water bottle.

Chapter Four

The sun had set, the day had turned to dusk. Jan walked from the office door over to the stairwell up to the apartment. She stopped when she heard Lee call out to her from the breezeway leading to the utility room.

"All done?"

"All done," said Jan. "You?"

"Ready to call it a day." Lee stood beside Jan near the bottom step, looked about. "Emily?"

Jan nodded toward the top of the stairs. "With Mother."

Lee looked up the stairwell, as if he could see Emily and Mother in the apartment.

"Has she said anything?"

"Just that we shouldn't worry, that she didn't bring anything down on us."

"I suppose that's something." He started up the stairs. "Doesn't tell us what brought her home."

"I'd like to know if she's moving in or just hiding out," said Jan, following Lee. "Or both."

They reached the top of the stairs, Lee opened the door and they entered their apartment.

Mother and Emily were sitting side-by-side at the window. Lee started toward the hall leading to the bedrooms. "Mother," he said, mumbling. "Emily."

Jan stopped midway to the kitchen.

"Mother? Emily?" she asked, waited. There was no response. "Mother?"

Still no response from Mother.

Emily shifted in her chair, looked over her shoulder to Jan.

"It's all right, Mom. Grandmother is..." Emily's words drifted; she looked to her grandmother. "Observing things."

Jan stepped around and sat on the back of the couch facing Emily. Her expression was thoughtful, studied. She folded her arms across her chest, furrowed her brow as she looked earnestly at Emily.

"Your history gives you a connection with Mother that your father and I will never have."

Emily glanced to Mother as if listening to something said, looked again to Jan with a thin smile.

"Mom..."

"I'm sorry," said Jan. "We should have taken you out of there so much sooner. We just... we were too close, too focused; we didn't see."

"I was as blind to the real purpose of the conservatory as anyone," said Emily. She glanced briefly to Mother. "It was grandmother, reaching out to me... from the dark place."

"I know," said Jan. "And that is your connection, your history."

"I suppose that is so."

"It is important." Jan looked in Mother's direction. "She missed you."

"Yes."

"I missed you," said Jan. "It is good to have you home."

"It is good to be home," said Emily after a long pause.

Mother tilted her head to the left, continued to face the window.

"Mother?" asked Jan.

Mother's head straightened. She tilted her head then slightly to the right.

Jan gave a slow nod. "Of course, Mother."

Emily shifted half forward, placed a hand on Mother's arm. Mother's head straightened again. She lifted her free hand and placed it on Emily's.

Emily's focus was on Mother.

Jan's focus was on Mother.

Seconds passed in silence.

Mother lifted her hand from Emily's, placed it in her lap, her focus forward, beyond the window.

Emily looked from Mother to Jan, then back to Mother.

"I know, Grandmother," she stated calmly.

Jan turned slowly about, saw Lee standing just in the room, one step from the bedrooms hallway. He was watching Mother.

He looked slowly then to Jan.

Matthew stepped out of his room, wearing a light windbreaker. He gently closed the door behind him, walked to the edge of the walk. It was early evening, just touching on dusk. He stepped down, walked across the parking lot toward the highway.

The motel / café sign was just lighting as he approached. He passed beneath it, reached the highway. He stopped, put his hands in the pockets of his jacket. He looked in both directions.

There were no vehicles on the highway.

He moved out onto the road, walked across to the barren landscape on the other side.

Evening had drifted to night. Sarah came out of the café. She stood looking across to the lonely highway, to the landscape beyond, as Samuel came out and locked the door.

He turned about then and stood beside Sarah. He followed the direction of Sarah's focus.

There… the silhouette of Matthew walking across the landscape, coming toward the highway and the motel.

"He's late," said Sarah, watching Matthew's approach.

"So I see."

"He's never late."

"He is tonight," said Samuel.

Sarah shook her head, let out a sigh.

"I do not like this," she said.

"I'll tell him to be more careful," said Samuel sarcastically.

"Things are happening." Sarah wrapped her arms about herself. "*Changes…*"

"He's simply a few minutes late, Sarah."

Matthew had reached the highway, started across the road.

Sarah nodded in Matthew's direction.

"The changes are subtle, but they are there," she said.

Samuel grew thoughtful.

"There have been… incidents," he said. "Events."

§

Jan spoke in hushed tones, sitting side by side on the couch. Mother was at the window. Looking out on the night, she was watching Matthew walk across the lot toward the motel.

Emily had left sometime earlier, returning to her room.

"I sense foreboding," said Lee, looking over the back of the couch in Mother's direction. "She's apprehensive... something is bothering her."

"Something is troubling her, yes," said Jan. "But we cannot know with any certainty the reason for it."

"Emily. Her return," said Lee. "What that means. For us all."

Jan slowly shook her head.

"Mother's foreboding and the reason for Emily coming home may be related, but one is not necessarily the cause of the other."

"The conservatory is always out there, and they will never stop searching. If they found Emily and followed her…"

"She says no."

"The conservatory is resolute," said Lee. "Emily belonged to Dark Star. Mother belonged to Dark Star."

"The project was ours," said Jan. "Emily was the subject of our project."

"The project was ours? You know better than that, Jan. All bore the Dark Star Conservatory stamp; including us."

I understand the concept of intellectual property, Lee." Jan looked over at Mother. Her tone grew ever softer. "But they don't own us. They don't own Mother."

"Really? They would disagree. Their most important, most secretive, and no doubt most valuable project." He turned from Mother again to Jan. "Whatever the project was. Whatever it… *is*."

"They are powerful, and yes, they are resolute. But they are not all seeing." Jan looked beyond Mother to the window, to what lay beyond the window. "Their eyes cannot reach us here."

"So long as Mother..." Lee's words drifted into the silence of the apartment.

"Mother is strong," Jan said after a long moment. "Her *change* will stand."

"And if Dark Star followed Emily home?"

"She insists that is not so. I trust her. She is not without her own abilities."

"Perhaps that is so, Jan. Yet... what is the source of Mother's disquiet?"

Jan and Lee grew silent, looked in the direction of Mother at the window.

Mother slowly turned her head until it was in profile, silhouetted against the glass of the window and the night beyond.

She turned back to look out at the night.

Chapter Five

The early morning sun splashed orange and yellow and red across the landscape. Matthew was sitting on an outcropping of rock, taking in the view. Behind him, the ribbon of empty highway cut across the scene, the motel/café and parking lot beyond.

Emily was midway between the highway and the rock outcropping, walking toward Matthew. He appeared not to take notice, his attention focused in the other direction.

The world was still but for Emily' approach. She reached the outcropping, climbed it, scooted about and sat beside Matthew. They both looked outward, neither speaking for several moments.

"Nice view," Emily said finally, absently.

"That it is," said Matthew.

More long seconds passed, a half-grin slowly forming on Emily's face.

"Come here often?" she asked.

"Now and then."

"Yeah," said Emily. "Me too."

"I know."

Yes he did...

They had often seen one another in the distance during their respective travels into the wild, though they had seldom crossed paths beyond the motel and café.

"How goes the book?" asked Emily, breaking another silence.

"Working the final draft now," said Matthew. "Couple of weeks."

"That's great. I'm looking forward to it." Emily looked side-glance at Matthew. "Isn't this your writing period?"

"A few minutes yet."

"Right." Emily smiled then as she took in the scene before them. "I missed this."

"Mmm," Matthew acknowledged.

"You may not believe that, but I did miss this. This place; this…" The sentence faded into the surrounding world.

Matthew said nothing; Emily finally continued.

"I remember when you came to us, very early on," she said. "You fit right in."

"I was drawn here. We all were. But then, you know that." He looked directly at Emily. "And I do… believe you, that is; that you missed this."

He glanced back in the direction of the motel, across the landscape, across the ribbon of highway.

He looked again to Emily.

"How could you not? This world… it becomes a part of you, and you of it. It makes you more than you were, than you are." He grew thoughtful then. "I would think that to be separated from it would be to lose something of who you are."

"You have a keen understanding of... *here.*"

"As you say, I have been here for a long while."

"And you have a bit of the writer's eye."

"That too," Matthew said, shrugging.

Emily smiled and let their conversation drift into the surrounding silence. Her smile faded then, her brow furrowed almost imperceptibly.

But Matthew was able to see it.

"Emily?"

Emily's frown sharpened.

"Something is wrong." She shifted forward, slowly stood.

Matthew stood then as Emily turned about and looked back toward the motel.

"Grandmother..." said Emily, just above a whisper.

Matthew looked from Emily to the motel in the distance.

§

Jan came out of the kitchen, dressed for the day, cup of coffee in hand. She stepped into the middle of the apartment, took a sip of her coffee as she looked across the room to the window. Mother was sitting in her chair, looking outward. On the TV tray beside her was a cup, a small dish with breakfast cookies, a glass of water and her pill bottles.

Jan took another sip from her coffee, turned away.

Mother shifted her shoulders, tilted her head.

Beyond the window... a strange sedan moved along the hallway. It slowed, turned into the parking lot.

Jan sensed something... she stopped, turned back around and looked at Mother. She took several steps toward the window.

"Mother?" she asked, concerned. She took another step. "Mother? How is that possible?"

She came the rest of the way and stood beside Mother, looked through the window.

"But they can't..." she said. "They are outside..."

The strange vehicle moved slowly across the lot, toward the café.

Lee came into the main room from the hallway. He was buttoning his shirt, looking to Mother and Jan.

"Mother?" he asked. "Mother, what's wrong?"

Mother shifted her head; sharp, short jerks.

Jan looked over her shoulder to Lee, wearing a concerned look.

"Somehow... they found a way through Mother?"

"Who?" asked Lee. "Them?"

"I... I don't know." Jan turned back to look out the window. "I don't know."

§

Sarah watched from behind the counter as the front door opened and three strangers entered the café, two men and a woman, all in their thirties, all dressed in simple suits. Samuel stood in the doorway to the kitchen, watched the newcomers walk calmly to one of the tables. They were quietly, carefully studying the café as they moved across the room.

One of them, Reilly, looked across to Sarah as they sat. He lifted a hand, indicating the three of them.

Coffee all around...

Sarah nodded uncertainly, stepped to the coffee station and picked up the carafe. She gathered three cups and walked around the counter and started across the room to the table.

"Good morning." She set the cups on the table and began to fill them from the carafe, pushed each to the strangers. "What uh... what brings you to our neighborhood?"

"We were passing through," said Reilly. He picked up his cup, took a sip. "Which wasn't easy to do. You are somewhat off the beaten path."

The woman, Jansen, looked across the room toward Samuel, who was still standing at the kitchen door. She lifted her cup to him in a brief salute, gave him a brief nod.

Samuel's expression didn't change. He betrayed no emotion.

The third stranger, Martin, looked from the others and up to Sarah.

"Menu?" A bit impatient.

"Um... we don't have menus."

"No menus?" A bit irritated now.

"We've never really had a reason for menus." She glanced over at Samuel, questioning, looked back to those at the table. "Um... breakfast? How about eggs, potatoes, toast?"

Martin frowned, looked to Reilly. He ignored Sarah, dismissive, and picked up his coffee.

Reilly gave a faint, almost sympathetic smile to Sarah.

"That would be fine," he said. He looked to Martin. "Mr. Martin?"

"Yes," Martin sighed. "Fine, Mr. Reilly."

Sarah managed to force a smile. "Great."

She turned from the table, looked in Samuel's direction as she started back toward the counter. Samuel nodded in response, turned about and went back into the kitchen. Sarah returned the carafe to the coffee station. She watched the group of strangers as she gathered together three sets of place settings; silverware and napkins.

Reilly, Martin and Jansen waited patiently, in silence.

Sarah returned to the table; the guests leaned out of the way and allowed her to put their place settings before them. The woman, Jansen, spoke as she watched Sarah work.

"So, miss... I don't imagine you get a lot of business," she said. "Do you? Get much business?"

"We do well enough."

"Really? Interesting." Jansen looked to Reilly, then Martin. She looked then up to Sarah as Sarah finished setting places. "Mostly regulars, I expect."

"Expect so." Sarah took a step back from the table.

"Locals..." said Jansen.

"Expect so. Some." Sarah started back toward the counter.

"Miss?" Reilly called out to her.

Sarah turned back, wary. "Sir?"

"Orange juice all around?" he asked.

"Of course." Sarah continued then, moved around behind the counter. She looked through the food-up window into the kitchen.

She exchanged guarded glances with Samuel, who was preparing breakfast for three.

"They're playing with us," she said in whispered mumble.

Samuel silently focused his attention on his work.

Sarah turned then and opened the small refrigerator under the counter, took out a pitcher of orange juice. She watched the strangers at the table as she set out three small juice glasses, prepared to fill them.

Reilly, Martin and Jansen were silent, looking at one another, no emotion.

Reilly slowly turned his head and looked directly at Sarah.

He gave her a slow, easy nod.

Matthew stepped out of his room. Closing the door, he saw Emily standing outside her room, looking out across the parking lot. He started to say hello, stopped though when he noted her expression. It was apprehensive.

"Emily?" he asked. "Is everything all right?"

She didn't answer. He looked out across the lot, following her focus, as he stepped up beside her.

He saw the strange sedan parked in the lot.

"Company?" he asked.

Emily still didn't respond, didn't look to Matthew. She stepped down from the walkway, turned her head then and looked up in the direction of the upstairs apartment, to where Mother sat at the window.

She looked outward again, in the direction of the café, hidden from their view on the other side of the motel office. Matthew stepped down from the walk and stood beside the young woman. Emily finally gave a glance to Matthew, albeit briefly, before again looking forward.

"They have found a way through Mother," she said.

"They followed you."

"No," said Emily. "They did not."

Matthew looked curiously over at her. She hesitated.

"I was well off the grid," she stated.

Sensing something then, she half-turned and looked behind them.

Jan and Lee were stepping from the stairwell, tentatively, even concerned. Seeing Emily and Matthew in the lot, Emily looking back in their direction, they started toward her, joined them.

Jan nodded toward the strange car. "We have company," she said.

"Yes," said Emily.

"They followed you," Lee stated.

"No," said Emily. She looked out, across the parking lot, across the barren landscape beyond the highway. "There is... something else."

"Mother says the same," said Jan, looking from Lee back to Emily.

Emily was listening to something the others couldn't hear.

"There is another," she said then.

"So says Mother," said Jan.

Lee looked warily in the direction of the café. "Should we...?"

"This may be a recon," said Matthew.

"What more do they need to know?"

"Okay..." said Jan. She started forward. "Let's find out."

The others followed.

The three strangers had finished their breakfast, were now finishing their coffee and juice. Their breakfast dishes were pushed aside.

Sarah approached the table, guest check book in hand. She struggled to hide her apprehension.

"How was everything?" she asked.

"Excellent," said Reilly. "Everything was just excellent."

Jansen looked up at Sarah. Her expression was a touch playful, while her words carried a shadow of foreboding.

"We shall recommend your café to all our friends," she said. There was a faint gleam in her eye.

"That's... great." Sarah held out the guest check book. "Will there be anything else?"

"Thank you, no. I don't think so," said Reilly. He leaned back in his chair. "I think we're good; we should be on our way."

"Places to go, people to see," said Martin, stiffly.

"Yes, of course." Sarah pulled their guest check from the book, set it carefully onto the table. "Whenever you're ready."

She turned and walked away, slowly, afraid to look back, to see what they might be doing.

Reilly looked from Sarah's receding figure to his companions. He wore a half-smile as he brought his wallet out from his jacket pocket.

Jan and the others were midway across the parking lot when they saw three strangers walking toward their car. They watched them get into the unfamiliar vehicle, a few moments later watched the vehicle pull away and move across the lot to the highway. It turned onto the road, traveled slowly away.

Jan started forward again.

"Come on," she said, led the others to the café.

Sarah was sitting at a table, appeared mentally drained. She looked up at those coming in, said nothing.

Samuel was standing behind the counter, holding a glass of water.

"Hello, folks," he said. "Sit anywhere."

§

Several minutes later...

Samuel, still standing behind the counter, responded to a comment, "They certainly seemed to enjoy their breakfast," he said.

"Lousy tippers," Sarah grumbled, walking across the room to an empty table.

"But they didn't say anything?" asked Matthew. He was holding a glass of iced tea with both hands.

"They said lots," said Sarah. "All of it intentionally double-meaning, nothing direct. They were playing with us, having some fun." She leaned forward, slid her forearms onto the table. She clasped her hands, looked down at them. "They'll be back. And they'll bring friends."

"It is no coincidence," said Lee, looking over at Emily. "You coming home and Dark Star showing up."

"Coincidence? Of course not."

"And yet you say they didn't follow you here."

"Still so," said Emily.

"And Mother agrees," said Jan.

"Yes," said Lee. He rubbed tiredly at his temple. "I know."

The room grew quiet.

"So?" Sarah looked from Emily to Jan. "Can you let the rest of us in on it?"

"Yes. Do tell." Matthew looked directly at Emily, sitting across from him. "Emily? I believe you mentioned something about *another*."

"Yes sir," she said. She hesitated, looked away from Matthew. "He's out there. He found a way through my grandmother."

"I don't understand," said Sarah, looking to Emily's back. "Who? How could anyone get through Mother?"

It was Jan who responded. "Dark Star is a big place, Sarah. A lot of projects, not just Emily, not just Mother."

"Are you saying there's someone out there better and badder than Mother?" This was not something Sarah had ever considered.

"Grandmother felt him out there, felt him searching for her, searching for us." Emily grew introspective. "And then... brushing at her mind."

Matthew spoke calmly, his tone observational. "And then brushed away Mother's change..."

"I would say that's a yes." Sarah looked about the room, finally shrugged. "Just sayin'; considering our recent company."

"This *other*..." said Jan. "He found a way through Mother, and our recent visitors came in to investigate. And now that they've had a look around..."

"We don't know when they will return," said Lee. "Nor what to do when they do."

"What does Mother say?" asked Matthew.

"She doesn't," Jan said decisively.

Emily shifted slightly. "Well..." she said softly.

All looked expectantly to her. Matthew leaned nearer.

"The, uh, *coincidence* that wasn't?"

Emily turned to look side-glance to the other table, back then to Matthew.

"Grandmother called to out to me. I was to come home."

"I didn't know she could reach out that far," said Jan.

"Neither did I."

"She didn't tell you why?" asked Matthew.

"I sensed only that it was important, that she needed my help. Nothing more."

"But once you were here? Surely—"

"She is unsettled," said Emily, cutting him off. "She wants my help, but I am uncertain what form that help might take."

"Strengthen her attributes," Jan stated plainly.

"Is that possible?" asked Matthew.

"I do not know. Perhaps."

"Mother must believe so."

Lee, sitting beside Jan, grew thoughtful, considered.

"We knew very little of Mother's project," he said. "As for Emily's abilities, I believe they would at the very least allow for the possibility of such a joining. How that might support Mother's powers, I cannot know."

"We would need to know more of what underlies Mother's abilities in order to determine that," said Jan.

Lee nodded agreement, then looked across to Emily.

"I wish we could help you, Emily," he said. "Maybe, now that you know more of the threat that Mother sensed was coming, your way will be clearer to you."

"We shall see," Emily answered. "I am trying."

Jan lifted her gaze upward, "As is Mother."

"Yes," said Emily.

"Yes," said Lee.

"Isn't it too late?" asked Matthew, more an observation.

Sarah agreed. "I was wondering the same thing."

Emily looked away from all.

"I do not know."

The world was empty but for the delivery truck traveling the desolate highway. Reuben's hands rested casually on the steering wheel as he guided the vehicle with very little effort. A gentle breeze brushed desert sand across the road.

Up ahead then... the Next Exit sign.

Reuben mentally noted the sign and made ready. A moment later, the world ahead flickered, as an image might flicker in and out. The sign and the exit itself flickered, appeared and disappeared, appeared again.

The image of the sign solidified. The surrounding landscape returned to as it had been.

Before Reuben could process what had happened, he had reached the exit. He quickly activated the turn signal, took the exit.

The side highway appeared normal.

Only then did Reuben have a moment to wonder on what he had seen.

Was Mother doing something?

What else could it be?

Continuing down the highway, there was the motel sign, far up ahead.

Charlene had one forearm resting across the top of her steering wheel. The motel sign was up ahead, still far in the distance. A quick glance to her dash, checking her speed... sixty miles an hour.

The landscape ahead and to either side suddenly flickered in and out. It only lasted a moment, then all returned to normal.

Whoa...

The motel sign drew nearer, the structures took shape as silhouettes on the landscape to the right.

She placed both hands on the wheel, slowed the deputy sheriff vehicle and turned into the parking lot. She steered the sedan toward Reuben's delivery truck, which was parked near the café. She brought her sedan to a stop, looked about as she put it in park. Reuben was stepping around the front his truck.

Charlene got out of her car and walked over to Reuben.

The sky flickered suddenly, bright to dark, quickly back to normal.

Charlene absently rubbed her arms, looked beyond Reuben to the world beyond.

"A whole lot of strange things happening, Reuben."

"I've been seeing wicked stuff ever since coming off the main highway," said Reuben. "Mother's doing, you think?"

"No. No, I don't think so. At least not directly." Charlene looked to Reuben. "But I'm betting she's face to face with whatever it is that's going on; whoever is behind it."

Reuben gave a half-shrug, "I don't know enough about the doings of Mother."

"You're not alone there, my friend. We're both on the outside."

"You? Come now, Charlene; you and your dad have been here from the start. You lived here."

Charlene looked over at the motel, looked to the second floor of the office building, to the upstairs apartment and the large picture window. She could see Mother's silhouette in the window, spoke to Reuben while keeping her focus on the window.

"Sure," she said softly. "Sure, but that didn't earn me an inside seat. My dad, maybe. Me?" Her growing frown darkened. "I didn't see what it was all about; just a kid glad to get reacquainted with my dad."

She turned her gaze from the window to Reuben.

"Then, I made my choice," she said, tapping at her sheriff's deputy badge. "I became an outsider by choice."

She looked back again to the apartment window.

Mother could see Reuben's delivery truck and Charlene's deputy sheriff vehicle in the lot below. Reuben and Charlene were standing near their vehicles. Charlene was looking in the direction of the apartment window, to her.

Mother's attention shifted then and she watched as Mike's mail truck turned off the highway and came into the parking lot. It moved slowly toward Charlene and Reuben.

She lifted her gaze from the scene below, looked outward at the landscape surrounding the motel.

Matthew and Emily stood to one side, near their table, in a quiet exchange. Sarah started to the lunch counter with a tray of empty glasses and cups. Meanwhile, Jan and Lee were sitting at their table, Samuel standing beside them, arms folded across his chest.

Samuel looked down at the couple.

"Suppose I should get into the kitchen, get lunch going," he said. "You folks needing anything before I get started?"

"Thank you, no, Samuel," said Lee. "Don't mind us. We'll be getting out of your way."

Matthew looked from Emily across to the other conversation.

"I know I'll be taking what little is left of the morning to wrap my brain around all this." He took a step toward the door, looked back to Emily then. "Emily?"

"I'll walk with you," she answered.

They continued to the door as Samuel started toward the kitchen. Matthew unlocked the front door; he opened it. They had to step to one side, however, as Reuben stepped through, Charlene and Mike following him in.

"Excuse me," said Reuben, passing Matthew and Emily and entering the café.

Matthew gave an absentminded nod in answer as he and Emily started again to the door.

"Something we said?" Mike asked playfully.

"Sorry, Mike," said Matthew, looking back into the room. "Bit distracted."

"Uh, huh."

"I'll see you later." Matthew followed Emily out the door.

Sarah had begun clearing tables, looked up at the new arrivals as she moved from one table to the next.

"Good news and bad news, folks," she said. "Good news, I'll be ready to take your orders in just a minute. Pick a table. Water all around?"

Chapter Six

Lee was sitting in a folding chair outside the motel office, leaning back, quietly taking in the evening. This was something rare for Lee, but these were rare times.

He watched Matthew walking across the parking lot from the highway. When Matthew noticed Lee, he shifted direction and approached, gave a smile and half nod when he was close enough to talk without having to raise his voice.

"Good evening, Lee."

"Matthew."

Matthew stepped up beside Lee, turned and leaned back against the wall. He folded his arms across his chest.

"Pleasant out," he said.

"Pleasant enough."

"So..." Matthew said in a low sigh. "How's everyone holding up?"

"Don't really know. Folks mostly keeping to themselves," said Lee. "I expect they're doing all right."

"Yeah. Expect so." There was a long moment of quiet as Matthew gave a slow nod, casually watching the evening pass before them. "It's who we are, isn't it? It's how we ended up here. Why we were chosen."

"No way of knowing, really, why Mother chose one and not another; how she knew you and not another; what did she see, how did she..." Lee shrugged.

Matthew was looking across the lot to the highway.

"I was coming back from a conference... one more conference. I hadn't seen another car for miles. I saw the exit sign, was drawn to it. I just knew..."

"So did Jan," said Lee, knowing. "Mother brought us here, but it was Jan who knew this was it."

"Not you?"

"Oh sure, sure," said Lee. "But this is Jan's doing. Not mine, really. Not even Mother's, truth be told."

They both let that last settle into the silence for several moments.

"Don't get me wrong," Lee continued, then. "This is home for me. I can imagine no other. It's just that, well, let's just say this is Jan's show."

"I see that." Matthew had a half-smile.

"No doubt." Lee leaned back in his chair. "I don't mind. I do my job, whatever Jan says that is. I'm content."

"As are we all. It's kind of the point of this."

Another long pause as Lee considered.

"I hadn't thought of that," he said at last.

There was something in his tone. Matthew looked down at Lee. Lee appeared a bit unsettled, though he was trying to hide it.

"We'll be fine, Lee."

"And you base this on...?"

"Oh..." Matthew sighed, returned his focus to the landscape before them. "Mother's determination and Emily's *pluckiness.*"

"Yeah. There is that," said Lee. He thought a moment, then gave a sharp nod. "And then there's Jan."

"Exactly. There's Jan." Matthew sighed. "And my room is paid to the end of the month."

Lee appeared more relaxed now, He continued to stare outward.

"And we appreciate your diligence."

They both fell silent then, becoming one with the evening.

Midmorning. Jan was outside Room 6, Mr. Howard's room. She was returning supplies to the side pockets of her housekeeping cart, having finished cleaning Mr. Howard's room.

She glanced up briefly at Lee, approaching from the direction of the office.

"Nice morning," said Lee, glancing about. "Can you use some help?"

"I'm good," said Jan without looking up. "Morning chores done?"

"Wasn't much to do." Lee gave a long sigh, looked side-glance at Jan. "Maybe I'll go fishing."

Jan straightened, looked across her cart to Lee.

"Really..." she said matter-of-factly.

"Do I have a fishing pole?" he asked, looking outward, studying the landscape before them. "Is there a lake around here?"

He looked side-glance then to Jan, a half-smirk.

"Do I fish?"

"Not even ever..." Jan said calmly.

"Ah..." He let that sit a few moments. "Basketball. Do I have a basketball?"

Jan wore a kind smile, said nothing.

Lee took that as a no. He looked to Mr. Howard's closed door.

"And how is Mr. Howard this morning?"

Jan grew thoughtful, considered. She frowned.

"He's uncomfortable with what's going on. He's not saying it in so many words, but it's pretty clear."

"Sad. Really. So not him. He's always been the antithesis of uncomfortable."

Jan nodded, looking sadly at the door to Room 6.

"So one with this place," she said. "Perhaps more so than any of us. Always so... settled. He just... fits."

Both now appeared somber. Lee spoke in a quiet, confidential tone.

"What happens to him if, you know, things go bad?"

Jan turned from the door and looked down the row of rooms.

"This is his home," she said. "Our home."

That doesn't really answer the question... thought Lee.

"Right," he sighed. "Jan. That doesn't—"

"No," she stated absently. "I don't suppose it does."

Emily reached across to the TV tray and picked up her coffee. She took a sip, set the cup back on the tray, beside Mother's glass of water, her two pill bottles and dish of cookies. She looked over the tray to her grandmother.

"Time for your meds, Grandmother," she said, turned her focus to the view beyond the window.

Mother said nothing... at least, nothing aloud.

"Fine," said Emily. "I'm not your keeper."

Another long moment, then a faint smile formed on Emily's otherwise blank expression, this from something subvocal going on between them.

The rare hint of a smile formed on Mother's face. It lasted only a moment, then a return to Mother's expressionless state.

Emily sensed something... she half-turned to look at her grandmother.

Mother took a long, slow breath, her focus remaining beyond the window.

Emily again looked out...

Fade then to... empty gray... a thin, ethereal mist.

Close on Emily's hand, held out in front of her. She rubbed her fingertips together.

She lowered her hand as the mist slowly dissolved.

Emily was standing in the middle of a lonely county highway, the barren desert landscape stretching out to the horizons on either side. The remains of the light fog drifted across the road. Dark-gray silhouettes formed, never fully materializing. Emily struggled to see detail, but one by one the silhouettes faded away.

She turned slowly about then, taking in the otherworldly surroundings.

Fade back to...

Close on Emily's face. Her eyes were closed. She opened them... slowly. She turned her head, looked to her grandmother.

Mother was looking directly at her, her expression still blank, though her face was set firm.

Emily was back.

"Wow," she stated calmly.

At that, Mother slowly turned back to the window, returning to her duty watch.

The evening air was warm, the slight breeze keeping it comfortable. Sarah stood outside the café, taking in the evening.

Behind her, Samuel was locking the front door.

He stepped up beside her and they started across the parking lot in the direction of the motel. The row of rooms came into view. Matthew was approaching his room.

Sarah lifted her gaze up to the window of the upstairs apartment. Mother's silhouette was a dark gray shadow behind the glass.

"I don't want this to end," said Sarah.

Samuel briefly lifted his gaze to Mother, again to Matthew, who had opened his door and was just entering his room.

"I have every confidence that it will not end," he said. "Our presence here will continue."

They continued across the lot, approaching their rooms. As if sensing something, Sarah glanced back to the highway. The motel/café sign glowed dully above the lot, the road.

Emily was walking beneath the sign, having crossed the highway. She started across the parking lot.

Sarah turned forward again as she and Samuel reached the motel walkway.

"I hope you're right, Samuel," she said.

Chapter Seven

The apartment was dark. Mother was sitting at her window, the late night outside brighter than the dark of the apartment, the lights and stars and moon putting a faint shimmer on Mother's face.

She leaned her head just slightly back, keeping her focus beyond the window...

Fade to...

The walk along the motel rooms, aglow with the porch lights hanging on the wall beside each door.

The window of Emily's room; the curtains were pushed aside.

Emily was standing at the window, looking outward.

She closed her eyes...

Fade to...

A thin fog aglow with the orange, red and yellow colors of the rising dawn sun drifted across the highway in front of the motel. Emily was standing in the middle of the road, the ribbon of asphalt disappearing into the mist. As she watched, the shadowy silhouette of a man appeared in the fog, slowly materialized as the figure came slowly nearer; approaching, approaching...

The figure took form, the individual features became clearer. He was a middle-aged man, his salt and pepper hair slightly disheveled, as were his slacks, button shirt and light jacket.

He stopped three paces from Emily. He put on a thin, knowing smile.

"Emily..." he said.

Emily gave a half nod in answer.

"You've been looking for us," she stated flatly.

"Call me John." John shifted his gaze from left to right, tilted his head as he returned his focus to Emily. "Yes. I have."

His expression turned thoughtful.

"There are those concerned as to your well-being; the welfare of each of you," he said.

"Right," said Emily, the word a toss-aside. "Yeah, we're fine."

"That is good to hear."

A very long pause then; John glanced briefly about, slowly turned back to look sharply at Emily.

"It is time for you to come home," he stated. "For all of you to come home."

"Yeah... we're good," said Emily. "I think we'll stay right here, all the same to you."

"If it were up to me, not a problem. But it's not up to me."

They both fell silent again, each studying the other. After a few moments, the calm expression on John's face began to change, a curious look forming. He put on another slight, almost questioning smile.

"Grandmother?" he asked. "Interesting choice."

"We like it," said Emily. "Family bond and all that."

"I can certainly understand that. Maybe we can keep you folks together once we have you home."

"Yeah... like I said. We're good."

John's expression slowly changed yet again, this time shadowed with something akin to sympathy. He seemed about to say something, hesitated. He shifted his head... sensing something.

"Ah..." he said softly.

Emily turned her head slowly then, her face fading into a mist, fading to a shimmer of Mother's face. This lasted for several long moments. She turned forward then, the image of her face returning, solidifying. Her expression was calm, her eyes sparkling.

The landscape to either side of the highway faded, shimmered a light green, the green then darkening. Multiple shades of green, interspersed with shadow... evergreen trees formed within those shadows.

The ribbon of highway ran through a dark forest, the sky above the forest shading from dark to light.

"Impressive," said John, a quiet calm. A shadow brushed across his expressionless face.

He lifted a hand, waved it before him as he tilted his head. A mist drifted up the highway behind him, growing heavier as it came nearer.

Reaching and rolling over John, reaching and continuing past Emily, the mist became an increasingly thick fog. It drifted into the forest on either side of the highway, moved into the shadows of the forest.

The forest slowly dissolved, the hue of the dark greens growing lighter and lighter.

Browns and yellows and grays... the forming landscape slowly returning to that of the desert.

Emily's face remained expressionless. Behind her, the highway ran through a still forming desert landscape. She turned her head a quarter turn...

Fade to Emily standing outside her room now, her open door behind her. She looked outward past the parking lot to the landscape beyond the highway, her expression distant, blank.

Fade to Mother... sitting at her window, her face firm but unreadable.

Back to the highway then... to Emily and John, the landscape to either side fading from desert brown to blues and greens, the sky overhead turning a bright blue.

A lake formed in a park-like setting, surrounded by sweeping lawns.

Again to Mother, sitting at her window; shadows of blue and green swept slowly across her face.

Matthew stepped out of his motel room, moved to the edge of the walkway. The scene before him was surreal: across the highway was a landscape of green lawns surrounding a dark blue lake... but it appeared as a shadowy image, shimmering, not quite real. The sky was a deep, clear blue.

To Matthew's right, Samuel and Sarah were both standing outside their rooms, also taking in the scene. To his left, Emily was standing in front of her open door. She was staring outward, distant but looked distant, not quite there.

Sarah looked over to Matthew, then back to Samuel.

"What's going on?" she asked.

"Moving day..." he stated, overly calm.

"Moving—"

"Trying to."

Sarah stared at Samuel a moment more, then looked over to Matthew.

"Moving day?" she asked, maybe hoping to get a different answer.

"Looks that way." Matthew kept his focus outward. "Someone's looking to move us, someone else looking to stop it."

"Wow." She turned again to Samuel. "That's... troubling."

Samuel sensed her gaze.

"Quite."

Mother watched the slow, steady spread of the glow of the emerging dawn sun shimmering across the parking lot. Her head shifted slightly, though her expression was still blank.

Seconds passed, the rays of dawn shifted colors across the lot's gravel.

Mother's expression shaded from blank to the hint of questioning; her brow furrowed slightly. She turned her head, slowly, to look back over her shoulder.

More seconds passed...

Fade then to...

Mother no longer at her window. She was standing at the foot of the staircase. She stared blankly across the parking lot toward the highway.

The parking lot, the highway, the landscape beyond... empty, silent, faintly aglow with the dawn.

The ethereal ribbon of highway stretched across the barren desert landscape, the setting not quite real, the landscape not quite the motel landscape.

John wore a knowing smile as he took in the scene, looked again to Emily.

"This is quite futile, Emily," he said, keeping his smile in place. "Let us end this."

"My grandmother does not agree with the method of closure you offer."

"And yet here we are." He indicated their surroundings. "Wherever –*your grandmother*- sends us, here we will return."

"Yeah, well, we like it here. So, you know..."

"So you have suggested." John's smile reflected a hint of sympathy. "We know where you are, Emily. As you have seen, we can reach you. We <u>will</u> bring you home."

Emily took several moments to consider a smart response to that. Nothing came to mind.

"Home..." she said at last. "Most of my childhood there, yet... *home* isn't really the tag I would put on it."

"How sad," said John. "Everyone misses you so."

"Uh, huh."

John appeared ready to respond, paused then.

A thickening mist had begun to form well behind Emily. Above, the sky grew steadily darker, pushed nearer.

All was clear immediately around both Emily and John.

Behind Emily then, deep in the flowing mist, a darker mist formed; a shadowy silhouette that very slowly took the form of a human figure. As it formed, it drifted nearer Emily, stopping several paces behind her. It remained a shadow, iridescent and fluid, never fully solidifying, never fully recognizable.

John wore a knowing expression as he focused on the figure behind her. Seeing this, Emily sucked in an involuntary breath and stiffened her shoulders before she could stop herself.

"Hello, kind sir," said John, giving a brief nod. "Others doubted, but I was certain that you were near."

Emily turned her head slowly to one side, but not so far as to be able to see who or what was behind her. She kept her focus on John, and for the moment maintained her silence.

"They do not belong out here, friend." John's odd smile faded, his expression hardened. "You know that."

He hesitated then, his expression sincere, as sincere as he could make it.

"I promise you that no harm will come to them," he continued. "They are family. We will welcome them as lost brethren returned safe to us."

He studied the shadowy form.

"There is yet time," he said finally. "Consider."

Sensing something then, John turned his head, looked to his left. Though he tried to hide it, there was disquiet in his expression. Emily looked to where John was looking.

There... well off the highway, there was a figure in shadow. The form was not quite solid, yet it wasn't fully transparent.

It was Mother, standing motionless, her expression betraying no emotion.

She watched; silent.

John turned again to Emily.

"What is the phrase?" he asked. "The cavalry?"

Emily looked now from Mother to the figure behind her, seeing the shadowy presence for the first time. She turned forward, looked calmly to John.

"Overwhelming force," she suggested.

John's broad smile was stiff.

"Shall we see?"

The motel residents remained gathered along the walk outside their rooms. The world grew black: the sky and the landscape enclosing the motel. Heavy, silent.

As they watched then: sharp explosive cracks in the black sky, shattering across the dome-like shell hovering above the motel.

Far in the distance then, washes of color formed low on the horizon: red, purple, orange and green, appearing almost as watercolor.

The shell of sky calmed to quiet then, jet black.

"Can't say I think much of the new neighborhood," said Sarah.

"I don't think we're in a neighborhood," said Samuel.

"I don't think we're anywhere," said Matthew.

Moments later...

The splash of color laying on the horizon grew in size and intensity. It rushed toward the motel, the motel quickly awash in reds and purples.

More explosive cracks shattered across the black sky, accompanied now by explosive sounds of crackling thunder.

Mother standing at the foot of the stairs... her body jerked violently with each crack of thunder.

Emily standing outside her room, her expression distant. Her face shimmered in the reds and purples, the colors washing out with each bright explosion.

The cracks in the sky faded to black.

The world grew quiet and still.

"Okay," said Sarah. "What now?"

As if in answer, the distant horizon began to lighten; black shaded to dark brown, turned to light brown. Browns and yellows slowly swept from the horizon toward the motel, leaving the desert landscape in its wake; the sky slowly brightening to pale blue.

Realization set in among those standing outside their rooms.

"We're home, boys and girls," said Samuel.

Matthew silently agreed, glanced over in Emily's direction.

"Emily?" hurrying toward her. She had collapsed on the deck outside her room. He knelt before her, took her by one hand and pulled her up to a sitting position.

She nodded tiredly.

She seemed all right. Matthew glanced from her up to the others.

Sarah and Samuel had gone to Mother, were helping her to the bottom step of the stairs. Lee and Jan were clambering down the stairs from the upstairs apartment.

Matthew looked questioning again to Emily.

Emily forced a smile.

"I'm hoping they won't be bothering us again," she said. "Don't want to go through that a second time."

Lee remained with Mother, Sarah and Samuel as Jan came hurriedly over to Matthew and Emily. She looked quickly from one to the other.

"Emily? Are you all right."

"I'm fine, Mom," said Emily. "Grandmother?"

"She's stronger than all of us." Jan looked back to Mother, again about them. "Helluva thing, huh?"

Matthew and Emily looked outward, said nothing.

Jan looked back to Emily. "We're good, right?"

"I think so. For now."

Jan nodded slowly, absently. "Good... good," she mumbled.

Emily shifted about then and looked to Mr. Howard's room.

"Is Mr. Howard all right?" she asked.

Matthew looked confused, looked to Jan.

Jan's expression was equally confused. "Mr. Howard?" she asked.

"Yeah," Emily sighed, shifted about again and looked out across the parking lot, to the highway and the barren landscape beyond. "You should probably check on him. And maybe give him a month free room and board."

Jan looked curiously to the Mr. Howard's door, then to the window beside the door. There was movement behind the curtain, a shadow.

"Um..." Jan managed. "Okay, dear."

Chapter Eight

Mike stood in the open doorway of Room 8, the room at the end of the row. He was looking out across the parking lot and the landscape beyond, taking in the scene before him; this, his new home. It was early evening, the sun having only recently set. The waning day was still bright and warm.

Mike appeared to be in good spirits. He wore a pleasant smile. He was dressed not in a post office uniform but in jeans and a button shirt.

Emily came out of her room next to Mike's. She saw Mike as she closed her door, took the handful of steps toward him.

"Hey, Mike," she said. "Welcome to the neighborhood. All settled in?"

"Hey, Emily. Just about. Thanks." He looked carefully at Emily, his pleasant smile not quite as pleasant. "We're good, right?"

"We're good," said Emily. "Can't say they won't try again, but for now, we're good."

Emily stepped down from the walk and looked back to Mike.

"Come on," she said. "Time for dinner. I'm buying."

Mike gave a quick nod, reached behind him and closed his door. He stepped down from the walk and joined her.

"Thank you, Emily," he said as they started across the lot. "I hear the food's great here."

Morning...

Matthew sat at the table beneath his window, curtains pulled aside, coffee cup in hand. He looked at the glowing screen of his laptop. He took a sip of his coffee, holding the cup in both hands.

He looked out the window. It was a clear morning, looked like another warm day on the way.

He heard a sound then before he saw it... the housekeeping cart moving along the row of rooms. It appeared outside the window several seconds later, Jan behind it, pushing it along.

"Good morning, Jan." Matthew brought the cup to his lips, took another sip.

"Good morning to you, Matthew," said Jan cheerily. "How goes your day?"

"Couldn't be better. A fine morning."

"That it is, Mr. Bedford." She continued along the walk at her steady pace, passing the window. The sound of the cart's wheels on wood faded.

Matthew took another sip of his coffee, set the cup down beside his laptop.

He got to work.

~ end...